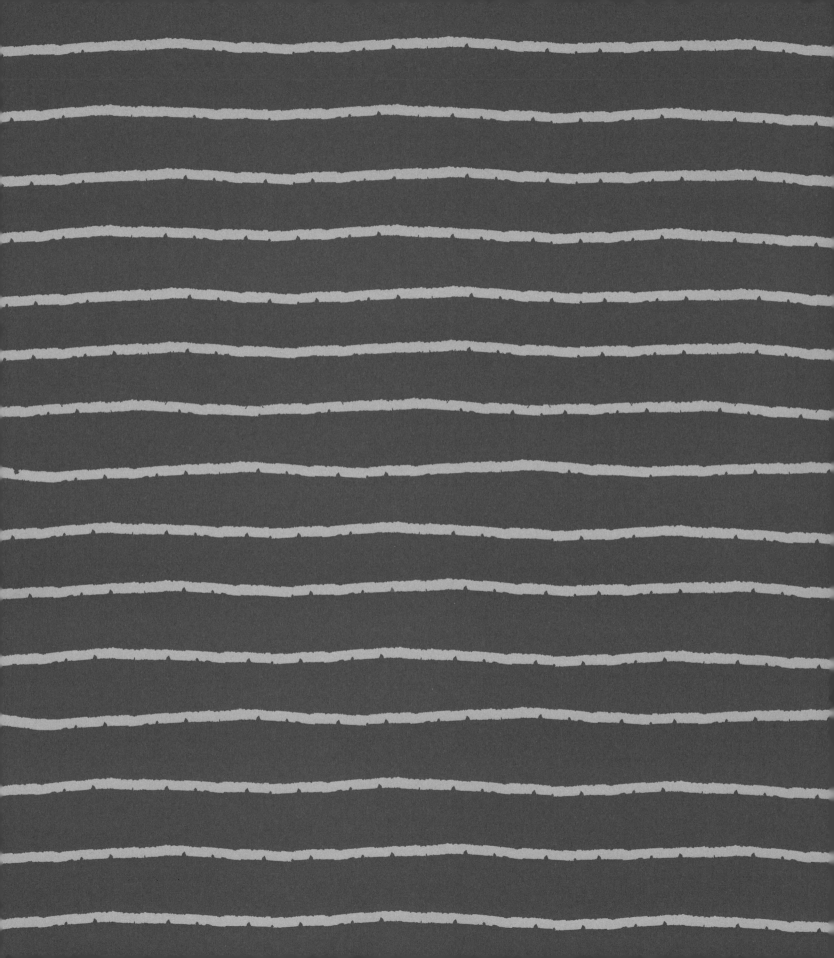

Bedtime Is Canceled

by Cece Meng

Illustrated by Aurélie Neyret

Clarion Books • Houghton Mifflin Harcourt • Boston • New York • 2012

To Dona AJ, for your compassionate support
of kids, for not being afraid to speak up, and for
always being the voice of reason—C.M.

To my family—A.N.

Clarion Books ● 215 Park Avenue South, New York, New York 10003 ● Text copyright © 2012 by Cece Meng ● Illustrations copyright © 2012 by Aurélie Neyret

All rights reserved. ● For information about permission to reproduce selections from this book, write to Permissions, Houghton Mifflin Harcourt Publishing Company,

215 Park Avenue South, New York, New York 10003. ● Clarion Books is an imprint of Houghton Mifflin Harcourt Publishing Company.

www.hmhbooks.com ● The text in this book was set in 16-point Italia. ● The illustrations were executed digitally.

Library of Congress Cataloging-in-Publication Data ● Meng, Cece. ● Bedtime is canceled / Cece Meng ; illustrated by Aurélie Neyret. ● p. cm.

Summary: When a newspaper headline says that bedtime is canceled, children everywhere rejoice. ● ISBN 978-0-547-63668-9 (hardcover) ● [1. Bedtime—Fiction.]

I. Neyret, Aurélie, ill. II. Title. ● PZ7.M5268Bed 2012 ● [E]—dc23 ● 2011041585 ● Manufactured in China

LEO 10 9 8 7 6 5 4 3 2 1 ● 4500372607

THE note read, "BEDTIME IS CANCELED." Maggie
thought of it. Her brother wrote it.

Their parents read it. They didn't believe it.

So into the trash it went . . .

until the wind got a hold of it. Up it flew, out the window, loop-de-loop, across town . . .

on the desk of a

newspaper reporter,

8

right on the pile of
finished work.

The newspaper printed it
in big, bold, black letters:

Today's News

NEW YORK, MONDAY, MAY 21, 2012

ONE DOLLAR

BEDTIME IS CANCELED!

tesque rhoncus nunc et augue. Integer id
Curabitur aliquet pellentesque diam. In-
s metus vitae elit lobortis egestas. Lorem
dolor sit amet, consectetur adipiscing
a vel erat non mauris convallis vehi-
et sapien. Integer tortor tellus, al-
s, convallis id, congue eu, qu-
rper felis vitae erat, qu-
s elementum
et tris

Pellentesque rhoncus nunc e
felis, Curabitur aliquet
quis metus vitae elit
dolor sit am
vel e

Everybody who read it believed it.

Even Principal Nancy at Maggie's school believed it.

And she was so surprised, she poured her morning coffee into her purse,

combed her hair with her toothbrush, and dried her face with her calico cat.

At school, Principal Nancy immediately sent a notice home to all the parents. The parents read it and were not happy about it. Some strongly disagreed with it.

A television reporter received an urgent text about it and raced to the school, where TV cameras filmed six parents throwing tantrums in the flower beds. Principal Nancy gave them a time-out.

On TV, the newscaster announced it:
"News alert! BEDTIME IS CANCELED!"
Everybody who watched it believed it.
Almost everybody.

E-mails were sent to friends to tell them about it. And the friends sent e-mails to their friends, who sent e-mails to their friends, who sent e-mails to their friends . . . The e-mails read, "Fwd: You're not going to believe this. BEDTIME IS CANCELED!"

Everybody who read it did believe it. By the end of the day, everybody knew about it.

That night, when it was time for bed, there was no time for bed. Bedtime was canceled. Pajamas lay unworn in their drawers. Bathtubs stood empty. Teddy bears sat on nicely made beds—forgotten.

Almost forgotten.

Kids played tag and hide-and-seek. They did some serious bed bouncing and wall climbing. Maggie's brother rescued her from the ceiling fan—twice.

TVs were left on, toys were left out,

dishes from midnight snacks piled up and up. Everyone was sleepy, but no one went to sleep.

Bedtime was canceled.

The next morning, tired moms and dads
were so busy yawning, some of them buttered
the dog's tail instead of the toast. Quite a few of
them served scrambled *pancakes* instead of eggs.

And one thousand twenty-six of them put on their pants backwards *and* inside out. Everybody was too tired to notice.

Almost everybody.

In school, Miss Klayborne couldn't
remember the answer to 1 + 1.

Mr. Jones got the ingredients mixed up in his science experiment and accidentally turned nine of his fingers green (and the tenth one pink). Teachers were so busy napping, they let the kids out of school late—very late.

This was noticed.

At dinner, fifty-six thousand parents fell asleep in their mashed potatoes.

Everyone was too tired to care.

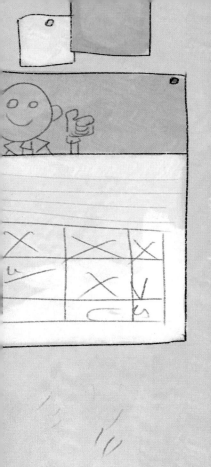

The new note read,
"BEDTIME IS *NOT* CANCELED!" Maggie
thought of it. Her brother wrote it. This time,
their parents believed it.

Maggie personally delivered the note
to the newspaper reporter. The newspaper
printed a special edition in big, bold, black
letters: "BEDTIME IS *NOT* CANCELED!"

Principal Nancy read it and called all the parents.
A television reporter heard about it and raced to
the school, where TV cameras filmed happy
parents doing some serious bed bouncing
and pillow tossing.

On TV, the newscaster announced it: "News alert! BEDTIME IS *NOT* CANCELED!"

E-mails were sent out around the world. Soon everybody knew about it.

And that night at bedtime, everybody went to bed.
Almost everybody.